DAVID MORTIMORE BAXTER

Liar!

by KAREN TAYLEUR

illustrated by Brann Garvey

Librarian Reviewer
Kathleen Baxter
Children's Literature Consultant
formerly with Anoka County Library, MN
BA College of Saint Catherine, St. Paul, MN
MA in Library Science, University of Minnesota

Reading Consultant
Elizabeth Stedem
Educator/Consultant, Colorado Springs, CO
MA in Elementary Education, University of Denver, CO

STONE ARCH BOOKS
Minneapolis   San Diego

First published in the United States in 2007
by Stone Arch Books,
151 Good Counsel Drive, P.O. Box 669,
Mankato, Minnesota 56002.
www.capstonepub.com

Published by arrangement with Black Dog Books

Library of Congress Cataloging-in-Publication Data
Tayleur, Karen.
    Liar!: The True Story of David Mortimore Baxter / by Karen Tayleur;
illustrated by Brann Garvey.
    p. cm. — (David Mortimore Baxter)
    Summary: A young boy relates some of the daily troubles caused by his
uncontrollable problem—telling lies.
    ISBN-13: 978-1-59889-074-7 (hardcover)
    ISBN-10: 1-59889-074-3 (hardcover)
    ISBN-13: 978-1-59889-206-2 (paperback)
    ISBN-10: 1-59889-206-1 (paperback)
    [1. Honesty—Fiction. 2. Humorous stories.] I. Garvey, Brann, ill. II. Title.
III. Series: Tayleur, Karen. David Mortimore Baxter.
PZ7.T21149Li 2007
[Fic]—dc22   2006005074

Art Director: Heather Kindseth
Graphic Designer: Kay Fraser

Photo Credits
Delaney Photography, cover

Printed in the United States of America in Stevens Point, Wisconsin.
122009
005645R

Table of Contents

CHAPTER 1

SMASHING SMORGAN AND THE TRUTH-BENDER

I'm **never, ever,** going to do it again. I know people say stuff like that all the time. But I really mean it. I don't have any **fingers, eyes,** or **toes crossed.** I'd swear my promise on someone's grave, but I don't know any dead people. I promised Mom that I wouldn't do it anymore. That was after I heard Mr. McCafferty tell her that he thought I should see a doctor.

"*That boy lies so much. I think it might be a medical condition,*" he said. Mr. McCafferty is our neighbor. He knows a lot about medical conditions. Mr. McCafferty watches every single medical show there is on TV. Maybe he thinks that as long as **other** people keep getting **sick, he'll** stay **healthy.**

My mother told Mr. McCafferty that I wasn't that bad. "*Davey just bends the truth sometimes,*" she said.

Bends the truth. That sentence made me think of **Smashing Smorgan**, my **favorite** wrestler from "Wicked Wrestling Mania." On one episode he grabbed Timid Truth, another wrestler. Then Smorgan gave him his famous half-pretzel twist.

That reminds me of the time that I told everyone at school that Smashing Smorgan was coming to our house for lunch. Of course, it was Rose Thornton's fault. **It usually is.**

Rose's mom is a PR person. That meant that Rose got to hang out with a lot of famous (and not famous) people. Rose never stopped talking about the people she wasn't allowed to talk about. **"You'll never guess who's coming to my place for dinner next month,"** Rose said one day. Some kids tried to guess. I looked out the window and watched the school janitor's dog unravel a toilet paper roll on the lawn.

"Who cares?" whispered Joe. He smacked my arm with my pencil case. **Joe Pagnopolous** liked Rose about as much as I did. Joe and I are members of a **Secret Club** that is so secret it doesn't have a name.

Actually, we just can't agree on a name, but we're still working on it. I looked across the room to see Bec rolling her eyes at me. "Boring," **BEC**'s  eyes were saying. Bec is the only other Secret Club member, and owner of **Ralph the rat**.

"I really can't tell," Rose Thornton said. "It's a secret. Mother would kill me." Just then, Ms. Stacey walked into the room.

"**Quiet now**, everyone. Time to do some work," said Ms. Stacey. She was wearing her grouchy **SSHH!!** face. I should have paid attention then.

"There really is someone coming to my place for dinner. **Someone famous**," Rose whispered at Joe and me. "Not that I'll ever tell you two losers who it is!"

"Who cares?" I said. I yawned. "It's not like you're the only one who knows famous people."

I looked down at my "**Wicked Wrestling Mania**" pencil case. An ugly face with a crooked nose and a cracked smile looked back at me.

"In fact, Smashing Smorgan is coming over to my house for lunch on Sunday," I continued. Then I gave Rose my best Smashing Smorgan snarl. Joe snorted.

"David Baxter, would you like to stand up and share that last remark with everyone? It must be quite amusing," Ms. Stacey said. She had her hands on her hips.

Rose Thornton raised her hand and waved it around as if she had something important to say, but Ms. Stacey ignored her. "Well, David?"

I had to STAND UP. And I had to repeat what I'd said. Rose would have told Ms. Stacey if I hadn't. A couple of kids laughed when I said that Smashing Smorgan was coming over. I didn't think anyone had believed me.

Until the next Sunday lunch.

I was sitting at the table with the usual Sunday crew — Mom, Dad, Gran, my sister, Zoe, my little brother, Harry, Joe, and Bec.

Bec nudged me and pointed out the window. A **whole crowd of kids** had gathered outside our house with cameras. Someone had painted a sign that read, **"We Think You're Smashing, Smorgan!"**

"**What?**" I said. I couldn't believe it. Bec shrugged her shoulders. I looked at Joe, but he wouldn't look me in the eye.

"What are those children doing outside?" my father asked, carving lasagna into big pieces.

"I think they're waiting for me to come out and play soccer," I answered. It could have been true. A couple of kids had started kicking a soccer ball to each other on the lawn. So it wasn't exactly a lie.

"Who's Smorgan?" asked Gran. She had great eyesight for someone her age. She was at least **120**.

"Uh, it's my nickname," I explained. "You know, like **Turbo.** Or **Scar.** Or **Spike**."

"**OR PINOCCHIO**," my sister, Zoe, whispered. She gave me a kick under the table.

"Who's Spike?" asked Gran. Once Gran gets on one subject, it's really hard to get her off it.

"I don't know. **Somebody. Nobody.** It was just an example," I answered.

"I had a cousin named Spike," said Gran.

The crowd of people outside started chanting, **"Smorgan, Smorgan, Smorgan!"** The kid with the sign was waving it around to try to get our attention. The soccer ball was stuck in a tree.

"Or was it Mike?" Gran wondered.

"What sort of nickname is **Smorgan**?" asked Dad. I shrugged.

"There's nothing wrong with the name David," Gran said, waving her fork at me. "*David Mortimore Baxter.* That name was good enough for your grandfather. He didn't need a nickname. You tell them. Your name's David." She glared at Joe and Bec. Then she broke a bread roll by thumping it on the side of her plate like she was cracking an egg.

"Morty, Morty, Morty," chanted my little brother, Harry.

He was sitting too far away for a kick under the table. I decided to deal with him later. Right now I wanted to know why Joe still wasn't looking me in the eye.

"Why are they **out there**?" I whispered to Joe from behind my napkin.

"I was STICKING UP for you," Joe whispered back. He took a sip of his drink. "Rose said she thought you were lying. So then I said you weren't. So then she said, 'We'll see.'"

"Why don't you ask your friends to join us for lunch?" asked my mother. She was serious. Mom grew up in a very big family. She thought nothing of cooking for twenty people, or even more. In fact, she cooked for that amount of people every day, even though there were only five of us. (Eight on Sundays, when Gran, Bec, and Joe came over.) **Our dog, Boris, had a weight problem from eating leftovers.**

"I'll go ask if they want to," I said.

The crowd outside was getting noisy. A small rock WHIZZED past my head as I walked out of the front door.

"Where is he, Baxter?" someone yelled. "Where's **Smorgan?**"

"Smorgan. Smorgan. Smorgan," the crowd chanted.

I held up my hands for quiet. "Smorgan couldn't make it," I said. Even before I finished the sentence the crowd of kids **booed** at me. Someone **threw a chocolate bar at me.**

"**Wait, wait,**" I yelled. I felt like I was on stage. Everyone was watching me. Near the front of the group, Rose Thornton stood with her arms crossed and her foot tapping. She was with a bunch of girls that the Secret Club called the **Giggling Girls**, or the **GG's** for short.

I knew what I should say. "Go home. I made it all up."

But I opened my mouth and something else came out. "Smorgan asked me to **invite you all** to a taping of 'Wicked Wrestling Mania.' I have to get the details. I'll let you know when I find out."

"In your dreams, Baxter," yelled someone.

"Yeah right," yelled someone else. It sounded like Ms. Stacey, my teacher.

"As soon as I find out," I promised. "**He's going to show us around the studio and everything.**" A whisper ran through the crowd. A couple of kids clapped.

Then everyone started to walk away in pairs or small groups. One kid ran up and got his chocolate bar. A couple of kids were throwing sticks into the tree to get the soccer ball down. The kid with the sign stayed and waved it.

"As soon as I find out," I repeated. I watched Rose and her friends giggle all the way down the street.

Inside the house, Gran was still talking about her cousin Mike. And Mom had just set the table for sixteen extra people.

As far as I could see, there were two ways to look at what I'd done. I might have given myself extra time to come up with a plan. But I might have gotten myself into DEEPER TROUBLE. Either way, I didn't know how I was going to get out of this one.

CHAPTER 2

DOG PEOPLE, CAT PEOPLE RAT PEOPLE

You've probably guessed by now that **I've bent the truth before**. I have. But it's not like I get up in the morning and think, "I'm going to tell some lies today!" It's not my fault. Things just happen to me.

Like the time when I invented a **new breed of dog** for the Hampton Animal Show.

See, I think that there are two kinds of people in this world. There are **dog people** and there are **cat people**. (Oh, and there are rat people, but that's another story.) Anyway, I don't mind cats. They're okay. But dogs are my kind of animals. Take my dog, Boris. Boris is **short** and **round** and **brown**. He's so slow and solid that my Gran once put her feet on him. She thought he was a footstool.

Sometimes Dad decides that Boris needs exercise. He pulls Boris off the couch, grabs a leash, grabs me, and then we go for a walk. When Dad takes Boris for a walk, it's a serious thing.

But when I take Boris for a walk, it's more of a fun thing. Usually we just go around the block once, checking out the neighborhood, and stop by Joe's house or Bec's house for something to eat.

It was on one of these short fun walks that the Hampton Animal Show problem began. Boris and I were just walking along, minding our own business. The next thing I knew, Boris was tugging at his leash and DRAGGING me across the road. He dragged me right into the path of Rose Thornton and her GG's.

Rose was holding a cell phone to her ear, trying to look important. "Hey, watch it," she said, as Boris tried wrapping his leash around her legs.

"Heel," I said. I tugged on Boris's leash. "Heel." That's what Dad always said when he walked Boris.

"Can't you control your dog?" asked Rose. "It is a dog, isn't it?" She peered closer at Boris. The Giggling Girls hooted and honked like geese.

Then I noticed that Rose was holding a dog leash too. At the end of the leash was the **skinniest dog** I'd ever seen. It looked like a balloon. One that still needed to be blown up.

One of the girls pointed to Boris and asked, "What's his name?"

"Boris," I said, feeling my neck turn red. "Boris Baxter. Heel," I told Boris as he stared at his new dog friend.

"Keep your dog away from my princess. Tiffany doesn't want fleas," Rose said, turning her nose up. Boris was checking out an overturned garbage can. The Giggling Girls, Rose Thornton, and I watched as Boris chewed on some bacon and empty eggshells.

"EWWW," sang the Giggling Girls in disgust.

By this time, Boris had given up on the bin and was trying to introduce himself to Tiffany. Tiffany was playing hard to get, but Boris was showing off, with slobber hanging out of both sides of his mouth. You could tell that Tiffany was impressed by the slight wag of her tail.

"Get your disgusting mutt away," said Rose as she pulled Tiffany closer.

"He's not disgusting," I said as I tried to pull Boris away.

"He's gross," said Rose.

"No **he's not**. And he's not a *MUTT*," I said.

"He's not? Then what breed is he?" Rose asked. She looked down her nose at Boris.

It was a good question. Boris isn't one kind of dog. He's not even two kinds of dog. Boris is about forty kinds of dogs. I looked down at his squashed face and curly coat. Boris looked back.

"Boris is a **Bullydoodle**," I lied.

"A what?" said Rose.

"It's a special kind of breed. **A cross between a bulldog and a poodle.** They're very *RARE*."

"Oh come on," Rose began. Then Tiffany barked at Boris and pranced around like a pony. Boris raced around the garbage can three times and then peed on Rose's leg with excitement.

I spent the rest of the afternoon at Joe's house.

That night, during the **torture** also called Mom's vegetarian loaf, my sister, Zoe, was looking pretty pleased with herself.

"Your *girlfriend* dropped by today, **Dribbles**," she said.

Dribbles was Zoe's nickname for me when I was a baby. Now she just calls me that to annoy me.

"Girlfriend?" asked Dad. He was pushing the veggie loaf around his plate.

"Rose Thornton," said Zoe, raising her arms like an actress.

"**Ooooooh,**" said Harry, rolling his eyes.

"As if," I said. I stuck my fork in the loaf.

"I think it's nice that David has girlfriends," said Mom.

"**She's not my girlfriend!**" I yelled. The veggie loaf slipped out from under my fork. Then it shot across the table onto Harry's plate.

"Mom, David's playing with his food," whined Harry. He was feeding his veggie loaf to Boris under the table.

"*That's enough, David,*" Mom said.

"Well, she's NOT my girlfriend! I don't have a girlfriend," I said. Harry put my slice back onto my plate.

"Aren't you friends with Bec anymore?" asked Zoe sweetly.

"Of course I am."

"But Bec's a girl."

I stabbed my veggie loaf again and we all watched **it zoom** across the table. It fell onto the floor, and then BOUNCED onto Boris's head.

"David! That is quite enough. I will not allow this behavior at the dinner table. I have better things to do than cook all day so you can play with your food."

"It was an accident!" I protested.

"Don't talk back! And since Harry brought it up, Rose Thornton did stop by today. With her mother." Mom gave me a look.

"Oh."

"Oh indeed. I was going to wait until after dinner to have this talk. Especially since veggie loaf is your *father's favorite meal*."

I looked at Dad. He seemed as SURPRISED as I was.

"I don't know how you trained Boris to perform that little trick, but *Mrs. Thornton is very upset*," continued Mom. "And so is Rose. You'll have to **pay** for her jeans to be dry cleaned."

"Boris knows a party trick?" asked Dad, looking interested.

"But, Mom!"

"Don't talk back! Honestly, David, you just can't seem to stay out of trouble lately. I don't know what's come over you. What do you have to say for yourself?"

"Mom!"

"That's enough. I don't want to hear another word. Go to your room."

Sending me to my room during dinner was a very BIG DEAL for Mom. She just hates the thought of anyone being hungry.

I walked out, happy to see Zoe and Harry's scowling faces left behind.

"Well, that's just more for us. *Who wants more veggie loaf?*" asked Mom.

* * *

After meeting Boris, Rose had to prove there was no such thing as a **Bullydoodle**. The next day in class, Ms. Stacey asked for an answer to a math problem. Rose raised her hand.

"Yes, Rose?" said Ms. Stacey.

"I was just wondering, Ms. Stacey, if there is such a thing as a **Bullydoodle dog**?" Rose asked.

Across the room, Bec snorted. Even the GG's LAUGHED in the back row.

"That's enough," said Ms. Stacey. "Do you have the answer to my question, Rose? No? Then please stay quiet."

Rose's cheeks turned BRIGHT RED — almost as red as her hair.

"You're a big liar, David Baxter," Rose whispered to me. "And soon everyone's going to know it."

That afternoon our class had study time in the library. Rose was talking in a loud voice and everyone could hear what she was saying. "Can you find anything about Bullydoodles in that book, Alana?" she asked loudly. "I can't find anything about them either. Anyway, you know how Tiffany is a purebred greyhound? Well, she cost Mother a fortune."

Next to me, Bec made a gagging sound.

"In fact, Mother is entering Tiffany into the Hampton Animal Show. Of course it wouldn't be fair to the other dogs . . ." And on and on and on Rose went.

At the end of library Rose passed me a note. It said, "Liar!"

"She's up to something," I said.

"Who?" asked Joe.

"Rose Thornton. She's **up to something**. I just wish I knew what it was."

I soon found out what it was. Rose Thornton had **entered Boris in the Hampton Animal Show.** When I walked into the kitchen after school, the entry form, addressed to Mom, was on the kitchen table.

It was time for a **Secret Club** meeting.

* * *

"Is this an official Secret Club meeting?" asked Bec on the phone.

"**Yep.**"

"Okay. I'll bring **THE BOOK** ," said Bec. Then she hung up loudly in my ear.

Bec was the **keeper** of **The Book**. The book was her idea and she was very careful about keeping every meeting recorded, and every who-said-what written down. Which is kind of funny if you'd ever seen how messy Bec can be with her homework.

We **didn't** have a Secret Club headquarters. This time we held our meeting in the pantry at my house. I thought the Baxter pantry was perfect. There was a light, it was private, and it **had lots of food** in case we got hungry.

We sat on the floor and got comfortable.

"**I call this meeting to order,**" I began.

"Could you pass me a granola bar?" Joe asked.

"Should I write that down?" Bec asked, scribbling on the Club Book and trying to get her pen to work.

"No," I answered grumpily. I reached for the granola bars and a pile of dried peas and beans boxes fell off of the shelf, hitting my head.

We were all quiet. I could hear a SCRATCHING noise outside the pantry door.

"Do you have rats?" asked Bec, suddenly interested. **Rats were her favorite animals.**

A sudden heavy breathing through the crack of the door raised the hairs on my neck.

"**Quiet**," I commanded.

We listened as the breathing continued. In.
Out. In. Out.

"Do you have **ghosts**?" asked Joe.

The breathing exploded into a sneeze. I kicked the
door open and found Boris scrambling to get inside.
Bec shut the door behind him. Boris lay down on the
floor, resting his head on Joe's leg.

"Does he have to be here?" complained Joe,
looking at the dog's drool.

"Well, the meeting is about 𝔅𝕺ℝ𝕴𝕾," I said.

"Really? What's the problem?" asked Joe.

"One word," I said. "**Rose Thornton**."

"Actually, that's **two** words," said Bec.

"Whatever," I said.

I explained the problem. The Animal Show. Rose
Thornton's prize pooch leaving with a first place
ribbon. Boris the mutt leaving in **disgrace**.

"We could switch him," said Joe. "I've read about that kind of thing happening in horse races."

"Switch him with what?" asked Bec. She tapped her pen on the club book. "Boris and Tiffany can't possibly end up in the same competition together. Tiffany's a greyhound. And Boris is a mutt."

"Bullydoodle," I said sadly. I admitted to Joe and Bec the truth about the new breed of dog that I'd invented.

"Well, there's not going to be a category for Bullydoodles," said Bec after I'd finished the story. "Maybe the judges won't let you enter."

"It's too late." I waved the form in the air. "Boris is registered for Event 12B. Special Tricks Event. The form came in the mail, addressed to Mom. She thinks I organized it. She thinks that it's a great idea!"

"Well, maybe you could teach Boris a few tricks," said Bec. She looked down at Boris. "If there was an event for **Best Drooling**, he'd definitely win first place."

"David, what's the WORST that can happen?" asked Joe.

"Rose can find out that I made up the **Bullydoodle breed**. She'll tell everyone at school, and I'll never hear the end of it," I said.

Unfortunately, that **wasn't the worst thing that could happen.** Not by a long shot.

* * *

The **big day** arrived. Boris and I were ready to go to the animal show alone. Mom decided to make it a big family day. She packed a picnic lunch, including her famous veggie loaf. She invited Gran, and even made Zoe come along. Harry said he wouldn't miss it for the world.

When we arrived at the dog show, I looked around. "Boris and I need to stay here," I told my family, POINTING to the registration line inside the big event center.

"Horace? Who's Horace?" said Gran angrily. I could still hear her complaining as my family walked away to get ringside seats.

"Next," called out an official from behind the counter. The woman didn't even look up as we stood in front of her.

"Name?" she asked.

"Baxter," I said. "Boris Baxter."

"I have your registration here," she said, "but there seems to be some information missing." She frowned and poked at some keys. "What's Boris's breed?"

"**Bullydoodle**," I said. I widened my eyes at Boris. He licked his face.

"Okay," said the official. She typed the extra information in and pressed the print button. A printer pushed out a piece of paper and a sticky sheet of number labels. "Keep these with you at all times. Please make your way to the **Dog Pavilion. Next!**"

Boris and **I** walked away.

The arena was roped off into three sections so that three events could happen at the same time.

Event 12B, which Boris would be in, was in the middle section. There were ten dogs in our event. Everyone seemed to know what to do. Everyone, that is, except us.

"**Ormond Atticus — Border Collie**," boomed the loudspeaker, and our event began.

A collie dog ran forward. He sat. He dropped. He jumped over three small fences. He rolled left, then right. **Everyone clapped** as he went back to his owner. The judges smiled and made notes on their score sheets.

"**Boris Baxter — Bullydoodle?**" came the next call over the loudspeaker.

It looked like Bullydoodle had just become an official dog breed.

I began to wish I'd spent some time training Boris.

I heard Rose Thornton screech, "*What?*" from somewhere close by. I didn't have time to look at her face. This was Boris's big moment. I let Boris off his leash and he moved forward a step.

"**SIT**," I commanded. Luckily, Boris was already sitting.

"**Drop,**" I said. I pushed Boris's back legs with my toes and he dropped to the ground.

"**STAY,**" I said. Boris looked like he wanted to take a nap.

And that's when it happened. **Boris saw Rose and her greyhound Tiffany** in Section A. He got up and trotted over to say hi to his new friend.

"Heel," I commanded. "Heel."

By this time, Tiffany had seen Boris. She ran to meet him, **dragging** Rose behind her.

"Why did they let you in? Since when is a Bullydoodle a real dog breed?" yelled Rose as Boris and Tiffany began a **game of tag**. Boris ran under a judge's chair. The judge went **flying through the air.** Rose let go of Tiffany's leash as Tiffany followed Boris.

"This wasn't supposed to happen," cried Rose as some other dogs began rushing around.

A few officials even joined in the chase. It was nice to see them having F U N.

That night at home, Mom and I discussed the day's events.

"Davey, I don't want you to think that Boris isn't as good as all those dogs today. It just isn't in Boris's nature to be a **show dog**."

I nodded.

"But I'm really proud that you gave it your best try. Your father and I both are," she said, patting me on the back.

I nodded again.

"It's just too bad that Tiffany couldn't get her act together for Event 14A — Best First Time Entrant."

"It's a shame," I agreed.

"And it's just too bad that she got sick before the event," said Mom. "Though, I'm really not surprised. I visited the Dog Pavilion to wish the Thorntons the best of luck. I just wanted to smooth things over — you know, after that incident with Boris, and Rose's jeans?"

I tried **NOT** to smile.

"Honestly, Davey, I don't think the Thorntons ever feed that poor dog. It had the *skinniest tail* and its *little ribs* were *sticking out*."

"It's a greyhound, Mom. Greyhounds are supposed to look like that," I said.

"Well, *that's one greyhound that won't be hungry tonight*," she said smugly. She popped the empty veggie loaf container into the dishwasher.

Suddenly I felt sorry for Tiffany Thornton. If there's something I've noticed in this world, it's that there are **two kinds of dogs.** There are those that **eat veggie loaf**, and those that **DON'T.**

CHAPTER 3

WHEN YOU'RE RIGHT, YOU'RE RIGHT

You probably think that I'm **NOT** a normal kid. But if you think I'm weird, you should meet my friend Joseph Pagnopolous.

Joe's really lucky. His mom and dad own the **Pagnopolous Video Store**. Joe gets to watch all the new movies. That's probably the reason he wants to be an **ACTOR**. He's wanted to be an actor for so long, his mom finally let him take acting lessons. The problem is, Joe's always dressing as **his favorite movie character** — and his favorite **changes** every week. I never know who I'll be sitting next to in class. Like one time, Joe dressed up as a pirate.

"**Hello, landlubber**," said Joe as I sat down next to him. He was wearing an **eye patch**.

"Who are you today, Joe?" I asked. Before he could answer, Rose Thornton and her GG's swept their way into class. Rose stopped and pointed to Joe's eye patch.

"What is that?" she demanded.

"That's an eye patch, Rose," I answered. She gave me a nasty look. Then she turned back to Joe.

"Well?" she asked. Just then, Ms. Stacey walked in. Rose and the GG's sat in their seats.

Joe nudged me. "**Arrr,**" he whispered. "**That be a close call, me hearty.**" When Joe started acting like his favorite character there was no stopping him.

At recess, Rose found Bec, Joe, and me hanging out near the oak tree. Joe and Bec were having an imaginary sword fight.

"Well, well. If it isn't the *Three Musketeers,*" Rose sneered.

"The who?" I asked.

"You know. That DVD we watched. The one with Kiefer Sutherland," said Joe.

"*Who?*" I asked.

"You're starting to *sound like an owl*, Baxter," said Rose.

"Anyway, Rose. What if we are? **Arrrr,**" replied Joe.

"Are are?" said Rose.

"No. **Arrrr, arrrr,**" said Joe. "As in hoist the flag and **scrape the barnacles.**"

Rose looked like she was having a bad hair day. I wondered if she knew.

She gave her fake smile. "How cute. The little babies are playing pirates."

I felt Bec tense up next to me. If Rose wasn't careful she'd be **walking the plank** from the highest branch.

"We're not playing pirates," I said. "Actually, we're going to 𝕋ℝ𝕐 𝕆𝕌𝕋 for the school play."

Rose pushed her hair out of her eyes. "What? You? We'll see about that." She stormed off to check the play volunteer list outside the teachers' room.

Being in a school play sounds like it would be fun, but the teacher in charge, **Mrs. Tozer, is crazy.** There are **thousands** of rehearsals, after school and on the weekends, and the plays are usually some silly thing with lots of singing and dancing. No pirates.

"Maybe the school play would be fun," said Joe, fighting with an invisible enemy.

"Who wants to be at school on the weekend?"
I said.

"**Arrrr.** When you're right, you're right," said Joe,
jabbing **his sword** at me.

After recess, Rose stopped by my desk. "I didn't see
your name on the school play list," she said.

"What's your point?" I asked.

"My point is, that I knew there was no way you
three would try out for parts in the school play."

"**Scum-sucking scurvy dog,**" muttered Joe.

"My point is, that I was right," continued Rose.
"My point is that if you're going to go around telling
lies, David Baxter, *you won't get away with it.* This is
not some little game at recess. This is the school play.
People pay to come and watch it."

"People **actually pay?**" I interrupted her.

"I will, of course, get the lead role. My singing
coach told Mother that *I am really talented.*"

"**Arrrr,** a talent for boring speeches," said Joe.

"Maybe *you two* should *grow up*." Rose reached over and pulled Joe's eye patch, which was attached to elastic around his head. She let it go. It snapped back against his skin.

"**Ouch!**" said Joe.

"See you later, Bluebeard." Rose tossed her hair, and then bounced back to her desk.

The next thing I saw was a **speeding spitball** that whizzed past Rose's head. It looked like a **huge ball of dandruff**. Joe let out a hearty pirate bellow. Bec looked very happy with her aim. A couple of kids laughed and some of the GG's shrieked.

Ms. Stacey banged her book on the table and the room was silent. "Rebecca Trigg, Joe Pagnopolous, and David Baxter. *You will remain after* class and see me."

That's how we ended up with our names on the **school play list**. We didn't have a choice. The list didn't have enough names, and we were the perfect victims.

After we left, I called for a meeting of the Secret Club. Bec lived in an apartment near school.

Our favorite meeting spot there was the
laundry room. It wasn't a perfect place,
but the washing machines made enough
noise to keep our talks secret.

"I call this meeting of the **Secret Club** to order,"
I began. Joe had left his eye patch at home. He was
now busy checking out a red sock that had escaped
from someone's dried clothes. Bec was sketching a
rat in a margin of the Book. **Her pet rat**, RALPH,
watched her from the safety of Bec's jacket pocket.

"Order." I raised my voice above the nearest dryer.
"What are you doing?" I asked Joe, who was holding
the **red sock on top of his head.**

Joe's latest thing was "improv." Improv meant that
he had to go around turning into a tree or a turtle or
something. He was now waving the sock on his head.

"**I'm a chicken,**" he said, clucking. Ralph ducked
his head into Bec's pocket.

"Well, unless you want to be a **chicken dinner,**
you'd better pay attention," I said.

We all talked about how we could get out of being in the school play. I think Joe was looking forward to being in the play. Bec thought she could ask to help with the stage sets instead of acting. She was really good at drawing.

"David, maybe you could ask Mrs. Tozer for a **backstage job**?" suggested Bec. She waved at Ralph, who was peering up out of her pocket. **Peek-a-boo** was Ralph's favorite game.

"She'll never let him. She really needs some boy actors." Joe stuck the red sock on his nose. "What am I now?" he asked.

Joe was not giving the problem his full attention.

"**An elephant,**" I said. "Joe, there's got to be a way to solve this."

"David, I think there's no way out," said Joe, waving his trunk around. "You're **stuck** with being in the school play."

"What did you say?" I asked.

"I'm sure Joe didn't mean —" began Bec.

"No. No, he's right. He's a genius! **They'll kick me out for sure.**"

Joe waved his trunk.

"I don't get it," said Bec.

"Let me work on it." I stopped talking and watched Joe, who had stuck the **sock onto his ear.**

"What am I now?" he asked.

"A boy with a **red sock on his ear**," said Bec.

* * *

By the end of our first play rehearsal, Mrs. Tozer was convinced I couldn't act. I read my lines like a **ROBOT. I fell over some seats.** I got tangled up in the stage curtains. Finally, she cried, "*Enough!*"

Mrs. Tozer told me that she thought I would be a **perfect backstage person**. My job was to help change the scenery, open and close the curtains, and help the actors remember their lines. This meant that I didn't get out of being part of the play. In fact, I had to go to every rehearsal, even on the weekends. Soon I knew all the lines.

Rose Thornton was the **star of the show**. Joe was the **villain pirate**. Mrs. Tozer had been so impressed with Joe imitating a pirate that she'd written a pirate into the play. His job was to come in near the end of the play and try to **capture Rose**. Joe didn't have many lines to say, and he couldn't even get them right.

"**Arrr**, me hearty. And where. Do you think you're going?" he said.

"Excellent, Joe," said Mrs. Tozer. "But I want you to say, 'And where do you think you're going?' all in one line. Try again."

"And where do you think? You're going."

Rose TAPPED her foot. "I can't work under these conditions," she moaned.

"Now, now," Mrs. Tozer said. "Everybody settle down. Once more, please, Joe."

On the night of the play, **the band** TUNED up as the audience arrived. Everyone was running around backstage, laughing and talking.

The sets looked great. Bec had managed to paint a small picture of Ralph into the scenery and Mrs. Tozer hadn't even noticed.

Joe was walking around giving his best pirate arrrs and scaring the **GG's**. I think they secretly like it.

Bec decided to watch the play from backstage to keep me company. She'd brought Ralph into the theater in her pocket. **Ralph was very interested** in what was going on, and he kept popping his head out to look around.

The first half of the play went well. I only had to whisper a few words to actors who had forgotten their lines. My curtain action was really smooth. People in the audience clapped loudly at the right times. It was near the end of the play when I realized there was A PROBLEM.

"**I feel sick,**" Joe whispered in my ear.

"**What?**" I looked at Joe. His face was a greenish color. "But you're on soon."

"**Can't,**" said Joe. He was bent over, holding onto his stomach. "Must've been something I ate."

"But you have to," I said.

"Stage fright, Joe?" asked Mrs. Tozer. She patted him on the shoulder.

"Can't go on," said Joe. His face was SWEATY.

Mrs. Tozer tapped me on the shoulder. "Looks like you'll have to fill in for Joe," she said. She put Joe's hat on my head. Then she PUSHED me onto the stage, right on cue. Joe's cue.

I didn't have time to worry.

Rose's eyes widened when she saw me on stage instead of Joe.

"Arrr, me hearty. And where do you think you're going?" I said.

Rose SCREAMED. Then she screamed some more. She was pretty good. Then she screamed again and pointed at me. I looked down at my jacket pocket and saw **Ralph**, playing peek-a-boo with Rose. The next thing I knew, Rose had pushed at me to get away. I tripped over some scenery and fell to the ground. Ralph took off like a shot.

"Ralph!" I cried. I dove onto the stage floor, my hands out to catch him, but Ralph ran around me. Then the other actors figured out what was going on and joined in the chase. We were running and tripping over each other on stage. The band started playing the theme song.

Ralph finally sat still on the stage, checking out his new friend — a painted rat in the scenery. The audience LAUGHED and CLAPPED.

"I haven't sung my final song!" cried Rose.

* * *

Mrs. Tozer said it was the **best play** the school had ever done. She thought next year's play should be a comedy. Joe decided he'd be a film actor so that he wouldn't get stage fright. Bec said it took Ralph a long time to get over his first stage appearance.

Rose Thornton didn't speak to us for a long time, which was good. She did drop a note on my desk the day after the play, though. I took it to the next Secret Club meeting. "You are all in trouble," it read.

"We better be careful," I said. "Looks like Rose hates us more than ever."

Bec nodded as she patted Ralph.

"**Arrr, me matey**," said Joe. "When you're right, you're right."

And unfortunately, I was right.

CHAPTER 4

DEAD WRONG

Sometimes you can be **completely wrong** about people. When I think Rose Thornton just can't get any meaner, she always proves me wrong. Two days after the play, Rose proved how mean she could be.

Victor Sneddon is the last person you'd want to meet in a **dark alley**. Or a light alley. In fact, anywhere. Victor Sneddon is **king of the bullies** at school. And Victor Sneddon also happens to be Rose Thornton's cousin. After the school play, I knew Rose had something planned for the Secret Club. We were trying to stay out of Rose's way, and were doing pretty well.

About a week after the school play, Joe called a Secret Club meeting. We decided to have it at my place, right after school. On the way home we went around a corner. And then we saw Victor Sneddon.

"Watch it," said Victor. As he pushed past Bec, the **Secret Club Book** fell out of her backpack. Victor quickly picked it up off the ground.

"**Lose something**?" he asked Bec. Then he looked at me. "Hey, Baxter. What are you hanging out with girls for?"

I didn't even know Victor knew my name. I was about to say I didn't hang out with girls. Then I realized he was talking about Bec.

"Looks like we have a problem. Request backup," said Joe into his watch. Joe was wearing **dark sunglasses**. He had moved on from being a pirate to being some kind of **special government agent**.

"What'd he say?" said Victor, his eyes looking small and mean.

Bec held her hand out for the Book. "**That's ours**," she said. "Give it back now, Victor."

"Give it back, Victor," said Victor in a high voice. "And what'll happen if I don't?" he asked in his normal voice. Bec tried to grab the Book, but Victor waved it high above her head.

"Don't worry, Bec," I said. "I left **that** important thing at home."

Victor stopped waving the book around. "What important thing?" he said.

"Nothing," I said.

"What important thing?" he repeated.

"We have a **code red** here. I repeat, **code red**," said Joe into his watch. "Request backup."

"It's nothing," I said quickly. "Nothing important. Just a stupid map —"

"Map?" Victor asked.

That's when my sister Zoe came around the corner and bumped into Victor. For a change I was glad to see her.

"Hey," she said to Victor. "Move it, you big lump."

"He's got our Book, Zoe," said Bec.

Zoe GRABBED the Book from Victor's hand and gave it to Bec.

"Leave these kids alone," said Zoe, poking Victor in the chest. "Why don't you play with someone your own size?" She walked off, leaving Victor with his mouth open.

Then Victor looked back at Bec, his eyes narrow and mean again.

"RUN!" yelled Bec.

We took off.

We ran down the street, past Zoe, across the park, past Mr. McCafferty's house and straight to my back door. We were still HUFFING and PUFFING when Mom saw us through the kitchen window.

"**What are you children doing?**" she asked.

"Practicing for gym class," I said.

"Well, don't go getting your school clothes dirty," said Mom. We all laughed, and then grabbed a drink before heading to the garage for our meeting.

"What was that **story about the map**?" asked Joe.

"**I don't know.** I just wanted to get The Book back from him. Anyway, it worked, didn't it?" I said.

"Only because **Zoe** came along," said Joe. I pushed Joe for saying that, even though I knew it was true.

He pushed me back. Then the meeting started and I FORGOT all about Victor Sneddon. I didn't once wonder if Victor had followed us home. I didn't think about that until later.

It wasn't until the next morning at school that I worried about seeing Victor Sneddon **again**. As I got my books out of my locker, I watched him talking to Rose Thornton. **He pointed toward Bec, Joe, and me a few times.** Rose looked over and nodded.

"Looks like we might have ourselves a **little problem**," said Joe.

"Rose **set us up**," said Bec.

I nodded. Victor had known my name when he saw us on the way home from school. And I BET it was Rose Thornton who made sure he knew it.

In class, Rose stopped by my desk.

"Victor said to *say hi*," she said with a smug smile.

"Give me the info on a Ms. Rose Thornton. **Tallish, red hair, laughs like a donkey**," said Joe into his **watch**.

Rose ignored him. "Victor said if you *hand over the map,* he might leave you alone," she said.

"**Map**?" said Joe with a frown.

But I knew what Rose was talking about.

"Victor **KNOWS** *where you* live. He followed you home yesterday," said Rose. I looked over at Bec, who'd been listening.

"So what do I tell him?" Rose asked.

"**Spider!**" screamed Bec, scrambling up to stand on her seat. Rose Thornton ran to the door and the GG's shrieked. People stamped their feet and banged their books on the desks. It was a couple of minutes before everyone had settled down to work.

Ms. Stacey seemed suspicious about the spider. She should have been. I'd never known Bec to be scared of a spider yet.

At recess, Joe, Bec and I met at the oak tree.

"Now what have you gotten us into?" asked Bec. "**You've really done it this time, David.**"

"Hey, that's not fair —"

"David, Agent Trigg is correct," said Joe in his special agent talk. "The map story was in fact untrue. We are unable to hand a map over to Mr. Sneddon. **The map does not exist.**"

"It doesn't exist **yet**," I said. "But maybe Bec could make one."

"I'm too young to die," said Bec, shaking her head.

"Come on, Bec. You're so good at drawing," I said.

"You are," Joe agreed.

"And **we can rub some dirt** or something on it to make it look old," I said.

"**Coffee**," said Bec.

"**What?**" I asked.

"You dip paper in cold coffee. **To make it look old.**"

"So you'll do it?" I asked.

"Maybe I could tear some of the edges." Bec sat down and drew a map in the dirt with a stick.

"**Agent Rebecca Trigg to the rescue**," said Joe, watching Bec work.

I was hoping that was true. But I wasn't so sure.

After recess, I told Rose Thornton that Victor could have the map. Then I told her that it would take us a few days to get it.

"**It's in a secret place**," I said. "I can't always get there."

Rose just looked at me. "Do you realize who you're dealing with?" she asked.

"**It's true**," I said. "I just need a couple of days."

"I'll tell *him*," she said. "But you better make sure he gets that map. *Or else.*"

Rose walked back to her desk and Joe tapped me on the shoulder.

"Agent Baxter, everything's under control," he said. "What does **'Or else' mean**?"

I **SHRUGGED**. I didn't want to think about it.

A couple of days later we had a Secret Club meeting at Joe's house. Mrs. P. kept trying to feed us her homemade cake. Finally I called the meeting to order and Bec showed the map.

It was great. If I hadn't known better, I would have thought the map was REAL.

"That's **awesome**, Bec!" I said.

"**Good work**, Agent Trigg," said Joe.

"It's not bad," said Bec, looking pleased.

I looked closely at the map. Bec had drawn it on a blank piece of paper. Then she'd torn some of the edges and dyed the paper with cold, black coffee. The map looked ancient.

"**It's a treasure map**," I said.

Bec shrugged. "What else?" she said. "It'll take him years to figure out it's a fake. By then he'll have forgotten all about us."

"We're on a code green, here," said Joe. "**All systems go.**"

I liked Joe better when he was a pirate.

The next day, I gave the map to Rose, who passed it on to Victor. I hoped that would be the end of it.

Over the next few days I forgot about Victor. Which is why it was such a SHOCK to see him hanging around Mr. McCafferty's front yard the next weekend.

"What's he doing there?" I whispered to Bec. Joe, Bec, and I were hiding behind a tree in the park right across the road from Mr. McCafferty's house. We'd been playing soccer before Joe had spied Victor.

"I have a bad feeling about this," said Bec nervously.

"What is he doing?" asked Joe.

I watched Victor take a **small shovel** from his backpack. He looked around, and then hopped over Mr. McCafferty's low front fence and ducked down behind it.

"Is he **working** in the garden?" asked Joe.

Bec shook her head.

"Maybe he's going to **steal something**," I said. "We should **call the police**."

"It's the map," said Bec. "Victor's **LOOKING** for treasure."

"But why would he be looking in **Mr. McCafferty's garden**?" I asked. "It wasn't a real map. You just made it up, didn't you, Bec?"

"**Kind of**," said Bec, frowning. "I didn't put any street names or anything like that on the map. But I guess I was thinking about your neighborhood when I drew the map. Maybe *Victor guessed*."

I **GROANED**.

"Well, Bec. That's dumb," said Joe, shaking his head. "Now he's going to find the treasure."

"**There is no treasure!**" I cried.

"Oh yeah," said Joe. "So what's the problem?"

"The **problem**," said Bec, "is that there is **no** treasure. And when Victor finds out, *we're dead.*"

D.M.B

That night I came up with a great plan. I would bury some treasure in Mr. McCafferty's yard for Victor Sneddon to find. I emptied all the money in my moneybox into an old cookie tin. There was just enough to cover the bottom of the tin. Then I grabbed the dog leash and pulled Boris off the couch.

"I'm taking Boris for a walk," I yelled out.

"Come home soon, Davey. It's almost dinner time," Mom called back.

Boris seemed confused when we stopped outside Mr. McCafferty's home. I could see the flashing light of the television through the window. It was six o'clock, so he was probably watching his favorite medical show. I felt pretty safe.

I told Boris to be the LOOKOUT. Then I hopped over the fence. I could see the hole that Victor Sneddon had dug earlier in the day. I moved up to a bit of dirt under Mr. McCafferty's rose bushes. The dirt was so soft I could dig a hole with my hands. Everything was going perfectly until **Mr. Figgins**, Mr. McCafferty's cat, jumped up onto the low fence near Boris.

Boris started barking and a **large hand grabbed me by the collar.**

"What are you doing here, Baxter?" asked Victor Sneddon, who was holding on to me. Then the front **light** of Mr. McCafferty's house **snapped on.**

"All right. Stay where you are, you two," said Mr. McCafferty. "I'm calling the police."

"It's me, Mr. McCafferty. David. **David Baxter,**" I called out.

Mr. McCafferty peered out through the darkness.

"So it is," he said. "I knew you were 𝕅𝕆 𝔾𝕆𝕆𝔻, Baxter. And who's that with you?"

"It's Victor. Victor Sneddon," I said.

I looked at Victor, who looked scared.

"He's my **friend**," I said.

"Well, what **are you doing** here? And what's that in your **hands**?" asked Mr. McCafferty.

I looked down at the tin of money.

"Treasure," Victor said.

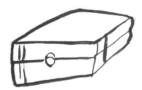

"**Treasure?**" said Mr. McCafferty. He walked over and picked Mr. Figgins up. The cat began purring in his arms.

"I followed a **map** —" Victor began, before I nudged him in the ribs.

"**Treasure?**" repeated Mr. McCafferty. A little smile lit up his face as he stroked Mr. Figgins. "That's no treasure. **That's my money tin**. I remember burying those coins. **Years ago**. You'd better hand them over and head home. And take that dog with you. He's scaring Mr. Figgins. I'll be **CALLING** your parents, David."

I couldn't tell Mr. McCafferty it was my money tin, because Victor would have had me **on toast for breakfast**. I decided that Mr. McCafferty knew it wasn't his tin, but there was nothing else I could do. I handed the tin over to Mr. McCafferty.

Victor walked back home with Boris and me. "How much money do you think there was?" he asked.

"**A couple of hundred,**" I said. "Maybe a thousand."

Victor SHOOK his head. "Well, neither one of us ended up with **the treasure**," he said.

Mom was waiting at the front door, one hand on her hip. "David Baxter, your dinner is getting cold. Mr. McCafferty is on the phone with your father. What did I say about staying away from him? And what did Boris do to Mr. Figgins? Is your friend staying for dinner?"

Victor called his dad, and then stayed for dinner. **I showed him how to feed Mom's veggie loaf to Boris under the table.** Victor actually wasn't so big when he was sitting down. And even though Zoe was really rude to him, I thought I saw him smile at her.

After dinner we hung out in my room for a while. I showed him my baseball card collection, but he seemed more interested in asking me questions about **Zoe**. By the time he left, we'd both agreed that Rose Thornton was a pain, and that Victor would leave me and the Secret Club members ALONE.

After Victor finally left, Zoe said, "Hey, **Dribbles**. I thought you two were **enemies**."

"*I did too*," I said.

As I always say, sometimes you can just be totally WRONG about people.

CHAPTER 5

REVENGE

If you've read this far, you should see that it **wasn't my fault**. The Smashing Smorgan thing, I mean.

When Rose found out that her plan to use Victor to get to me didn't work, she took *REVENGE*. Two weeks after the play, Rose raised her hand in class, even though Ms. Stacey hadn't asked a question. Rose was looking straight at me, so I knew I was in trouble.

"Yes, Rose," said Ms. Stacey.

"Ms. Stacey, I was just wondering when we were going to see Smashing Smorgan. You know, like David promised?" Rose kept her face still but I could tell she was smirking inside.

"Well, that's a **good question**, Rose," said Ms. Stacey. "**David**?"

It was the **perfect time** to do it. *STAND UP* and say, "*I made it all up.*"

I thought of the Hampton Animal Show **disaster**, which had happened because I lied about Boris's breed. And the school play. If only I'd said to Rose, "Yes, we are playing pirates," instead of pretending we were rehearsing for the school play, I wouldn't have ended up looking like an IDIOT on stage.

I knew what I should do. Tell the truth. It doesn't get any easier than that.

Everyone had turned around to look at me.

"Well, Ms. Stacey," I muttered.

"Stand up, David. We can't hear you," said Ms. Stacey.

"The thing is —" I coughed and cleared my throat. "I'm really sorry, but I just made up that story about Smashing Smorgan. He never was coming over to my place for dinner. I don't even know him."

The class was so quiet, you could have heard **Boris's drool hit the floor.**

I went on, "So, you see, we won't be going to see him —"

A **CHOKING SOUND** came out of Ms. Stacey's mouth.

"The thing is . . ." I looked over at Rose. She had that stupid smile on her face that said, "Bye bye."

"The thing is, I'm just joking!" I said. I stretched my mouth into a pretend smile. I saw the color come back to Ms. Stacey's face and ignored Joe kicking me to try to get me to shut up.

"Actually, the taping is next Saturday afternoon. I just need to recheck the time."

The class clapped and banged on their desks. The only person who didn't seem happy was Rose Thornton.

And that is how I found myself standing outside the Channel 13 television studio with fifteen kids from my class, plus Ms. Stacey. Rose Thornton was there, giving me her smug smile. **The Secret Club** members were there for support, hoping to come up with a **plan** to save me.

Joe was still in secret agent gear, but not even the government could save me now. I knew this was my fault. I needed to take care of it alone.

"I'll go in first," I explained to everyone. "Then I'll come and get you all."

Half the kids still thought I was lying. I knew I was.

Inside the studio foyer, there was a line of people with tickets waiting to get in. Official-
looking people were rushing around everywhere. **No one noticed me**. I guess I didn't look important enough to talk to.

The girl behind the ticket counter was chewing gum. She was wearing a black t-shirt with small gold lettering that read "STAFF."

"Do you have any **free tickets** for someone named David Baxter?" I asked her. I knew there wouldn't be, but I figured I should try. The girl shook her head.

"Do you have any free tickets for anyone?" I asked.

"Beat it, kid," she said. She looked me straight in the eye. I tried my best smile — the one I use on Mom so she'll buy me a candy bar.

The girl blew a large bubble then popped it. "Beat it," she repeated.

I was going to have to go outside and tell the truth. I went to the nearest door, which opened onto a long dark hallway. Which way was out? I walked down the corridor and stood in front of a door that had a **star** on it. Suddenly, the door opened wide and knocked me on my back. Now there were lots of stars — dancing around my head.

"Hey. Kid. You okay?" A huge hand reached out and pulled me to my feet. I felt kind of DIZZY.

The guy in front of me looked like he was three stories tall.

"Hey, kid. I said, are you okay?" said the giant. He grabbed a glass of water from his room and threw it over my face.

That's when I recognized him.

"Smashing Smorgan!" I said.

I told him EVERYTHING.

I told him about bending the truth and how it had gotten out of control. And I told him about the bunch of kids — and one teacher — who were waiting outside to meet my good old pal Smashing Smorgan.

Smorgan listened and nodded and **scratched** his **bald head** at times. Finally he twisted the ring through his eyebrow and coughed. Then he asked my name.

"David," I replied.

"David," he repeated. "David, sometimes **there's a fine line between telling a story and telling a lie.** You, my friend, have crossed the fine line by about a mile. You are in big trouble."

Smashing Smorgan grabbed me by the collar and pulled me to my feet. Then he marched me back down the hall and outside to the crowd of classmates, teacher, and Secret Club members.

I thought Ms. Stacey was going to faint. Her face turned white then RED then PURPLE then back to RED. "Oh. Oh. Mr. Smorgan," was all she could say.

The kids crowded around us. Smorgan tightened his grip on my shoulder.

"**Well**." Smorgan coughed. "Well. I just came out to let you know that **my friend David** has gotten the dates mixed up. For the free tickets, that is."

The group groaned. Someone yelled, **"Typical Baxter."**

"But if you'd all like to **come back** next week," Smorgan went on, looking at me, "I can **promise** you **ringside seats**."

Everyone **except** <u>Rose Thornton</u> cheered.

* * *

During the next week at school, everyone was talking about **Smashing Smorgan**. A few kids asked if I could get his 𝔸𝕌𝕋𝕆𝔾ℝ𝔸ℙ𝕳 for them, but I said he didn't like that kind of thing. Of course, I was only guessing. But everyone except Bec and Joe thought Smorgan and I were best friends.

Even Rose Thornton's gigglers were excited. They spent hours talking about what they would **wear** and how they'd **do their hair** and **stuff**.

I asked Bec how people could spend so much time thinking about dressing up. She just shrugged. "Beats me," she said. She was mad because Ms. Stacey had made her promise not to bring Ralph to the wrestling show.

Rose Thornton was MAD, too. It turned out that the famous person who was going to her place for dinner was just some dorky politician who had written a book and won some award. When everyone found out there were a few **oohs** and AHHS, but that was just people being polite.

Everyone had ringside seats for **"Wicked Wrestling Mania."**

Everyone, that is, except ME. Smorgan said he wanted to teach me a lesson.

My class and Ms. Stacey got to watch Smorgan smash his way to victory. I had to dust his dressing room, organize his fan mail, and clean his ten pairs of silver boots.

After the taping, Smorgan was happy with his dressing room. We talked about a whole bunch of stuff before I had to go home. In fact, **Smashing Smorgan is coming for Sunday lunch** at my place soon.

Right after we spend the morning sailing on the bay in my dad's luxury cruiser.

Okay, so here's the thing. My dad DOESN'T have a **luxury cruiser**. In fact, we don't have a boat at all.

The End

About the Author

When Karen Tayleur was growing up, her father told her many stories about his own childhood. These stories continued to grow. She says, "I always enjoyed the retelling, and wanted to create a character who had the same abilities with 'bending the truth.'" And David Mortimore Baxter was born! Karen lives in Australia with her husband, two children, two cats, and one dog.

About the Illustrator

Brann Garvey grew up in the great state of Iowa, where he studied art and visual communications. He graduated from the Minneapolis College of Art & Design with a degree in illustration. Brann is usually found with one or more of the following: a pencil in his hand, a comic book, a remote for watching DVDs, or his pet kitty, Iggy. When the weather is nice, Brann likes to play disc golf, and he proudly points out that Iowa is one of the world's centers for the sport. Iggy does not play.

heel (HEEL)—to follow closely behind

jeered (JEERD)—laughed at

mimic (MIM-ik)—to imitate, especially in order to make fun of

pathetic (puh-THET-ik)—sad

politician (pol-uh-TISH-uhn)—someone who runs for or holds a position in government

revenge (ri-VENJ)—to get back at

scenery (SEE-nur-ee)—the painted background of a theater set

scowling (SKOU-ling)—frowning

slobber (SLOB-ur)—drool

suspicious (suh-SPISH-uhss)—not to be trusted

tolerate (TOL-uh-rate)—to put up with

villain (VIL-uhn)—someone who is wicked or evil

Discussion Questions

1. How do you feel about "bending the truth" and "telling a lie?" Is there a difference? Explain your answer.

2. How does Ms. Stacey, David's teacher, feel about Smashing Smorgan? How do you know? What are some clues in the story?

3. Zoe thinks that a good nickname for David would be "Pinocchio." Why?

4. Was David wrong about Victor? Is Victor really a bully or is David the bully? Talk about Victor and David's relationship (in chapter four) and how it changes.

writing Prompts

1. David makes up a name for the breed (or type) of his dog. He combines bulldog and poodle to create a "bullydoodle." Can you create a new breed of dog combining two breeds? Give the breed a name, describe what it looks like and describe what it acts like.

2. What is a lie? How do you feel about lying? Write about why you feel this way.

3. What happens at your house when you or your family does not like a meal? Write about what happens and what people say.

4. Joe loves to wear disguises and act like different characters. First he was a pirate and then a government agent. Who would you like to be? Write about how you would act and what you would wear.

David Mortimore Baxter

David is a great kid, but he has one big problem—he can't stop talking. These wildly humorous stories, told by David himself, will show readers just how much trouble a boy and his mouth can get into, whether he's making promises to become class president or bragging that he's best friends with the world's most famous wrestler. David is amiable, engaging, cool, and smart enough to realize that growing up is the biggest adventure of all.

Internet Sites

Do you want to know more about subjects related to this book? Or are you interested in learning about other topics? Then check out FactHound, a fun, easy way to find Internet sites.

Our investigative staff has already sniffed out great sites for you!

Here's how to use FactHound:

1. Visit *www.facthound.com*

2. Select your grade level.

3. To learn more about subjects related to this book, type in the book's ISBN number: **1598890743**.

4. Click the **Fetch It** button.

FactHound will fetch the best Internet sites for you!